The Gift of the Girl Who Couldn't Hear

"Who would want to be a friend of such a girl," I think to myself as I try to button my blue jeans that fit when I got them this fall. "After all," I think, feeling worse by the second, "I am fat and bad tempered."

I used to get A's in school and this week on my midterm report I got two D's and a "Needs Improvement for Cooperation." I used to be the fastest runner in my class and now I come in third and sometimes fourth because my thighs, grown to the size of locomotives, slow me down. And until last year, I was the only girl in the whole school who got solo parts in the Christmas pageant, which is why, of course, I have thought all fall that I'd get the part of Annie at tryouts today.

THE Gift OF THE Gir

◆ ◆

Who Couldn't Hear

◆ ◆

SUSAN SHREVE

A Beech Tree Paperback Book
New York

Library of Congress Cataloging-in-Publication Data
Shreve, Susan Richards.
The gift of the girl who couldn't hear / Susan Shreve.   p.   cm.
Summary: Two friends, one of whom is deaf,
help each other when tryouts are held for a seventh-grade
production of "Annie."
ISBN 0-688-11694-9
[1. Deaf—Fiction. 2. Friendship—Fiction. 3. Schools—Fiction.]
I. Title.
[PZ7.S55915Gi   1993]   [Fic]—dc20   92-43763   CIP   AC

3 5 7 9 10 8 6 4
First Beech Tree Edition, 1993.

For Karena Levy,
with love
on her graduation from high school

This is not a true story exactly, but it is a true story inexactly. The friendship between Karena Levy and my daughter Elizabeth has been a gift to me.

CHAPTER

1

This morning, looking at myself in the full length mirror on my bedroom door, I come to a serious conclusion which I will tell you although I'd rather the news not get around Marywood Elementary where I go to school. The absolute fact is I don't like myself, especially in the mirror. Not even my hair which my grandmother says is my best asset.

I was thirteen on Monday of this week, October 15, and something terrible seems to have happened since last summer when I was a perfectly ordinary girl. Or so I thought.

This morning what I see in the mirror is a round-faced girl with freckles, pale blue eyes, black curly hair similar to that of a French poodle, and a square body which up until this summer was rectangular.

"Who would want to be a friend of such a girl," I think to myself as I try to button my blue jeans that fit when I got them this fall. "After all," I think, feeling worse by the second, "I am fat and bad tempered."

I used to have plenty of good friends—fourteen girls and three boys to be exact. Now I have none except Lucy, who is deaf and likes everyone in the seventh grade, but I'll tell you about that later. I suppose you can count my parents and little brother, Benjamin, who is only four, since my parents waited until my mother finished law school to have him. Not my brother Jacob, who is in the ninth grade and president of his class, of course, and captain of junior varsity soccer and drop-dead handsome, so the ninth-grade girls tell me, although he's shaped like a potato which is not my idea of good looks. Jacob has been telling me all of my life, since before he went to school, that he thinks I look like a Kewpie doll or that I'm bossy or simply that he doesn't like me. Yesterday he said he'd rather not walk to school with me until I look more mature, for which I hit him.

I used to get A's in school and this week on

my midterm report I got two D's and a "Needs Improvement for Cooperation." I used to be the fastest runner in my class and now I come in third and sometimes fourth because my thighs, grown to the size of locomotives, slow me down. And until last year, I was the only girl in the whole school who got solo parts in the Christmas pageant, which is why, of course, I have thought all fall that I'd get the part of Annie at tryouts today.

My parents are talking about me when I go downstairs for breakfast. I can tell by the quick bright smiles on their faces as I come into the kitchen and, besides, I overhear my father saying "insecure" and it doesn't refer to the cat.

Of course I'm insecure. I'd be crazy not to be.

No one at school knows the truth about me. At school I seem to be happy-go-lucky, a little plump and not as smart as I was in sixth grade. But otherwise no one thinks I have a care in the world except what I'll wear to school. I wouldn't dream of telling anybody the real truth especially at Marywood where the seventh-grade girls have just fallen in love with the seventh-grade boys and hang around their lockers whispering to one another. I have fallen in love with the seventh-grade boys too, but Jacob tells me no one in his right mind is going to fall back in love with me so I might as well forget it.

"So sweetheart," my mother says in her cheerful voice which tells me she's pretending to be happy because she knows I'm in a miserable mood. "You'll be home late today because of tryouts I suppose."

"Unlikely," I say, sitting down to breakfast next to Benjamin who is the apple of my parents' eye, to use my grandmother's expression. I know I am not the apple of their eye which is sufficient to make me feel angry at Benjamin most of the time including this morning. "I may not even try out," I say.

"Darling," my mother says. I can tell she is afraid of me because of my bad temper and so she responds with just "darling" to avoid trouble.

I don't want you to misunderstand. I love my mother. She is pretty and smart and has been that way all of her life. Nothing bad has ever happened to her except her father died when she was thirteen. So what would she know about the life of someone, even her daughter, who overnight turns unpretty and unsmart and mean?

"Of course you'll try out," my father says.

I shrug.

"It doesn't matter whether or not you get a part," my father says sitting down at the table next to Benjamin, ruffling his soft, yellow hair. "The important thing is to try out."

My father should have been a minister. He says all the right things and behaves sensibly even in emergencies. But instead he's an obstetrician who delivers babies, even some who are now my friends.

"I may be giving up singing," I say.

"Well, darling, it's fine if you don't want to try out," my mother says. "But Lucy's mother called earlier to say that she is trying out for *Annie* and perhaps she could go to tryouts with you."

"Lucy?" I say, completely amazed.

"That's what her mother says."

I should tell you that Lucy is completely deaf and has been since the moment she was born three days before me in 1977, although they didn't know she was deaf at the time. The way she understands people is by reading their lips, so you have to be face to face with her for her to know what you're saying. She can talk but her voice doesn't sound like other people's because she's never heard conversation.

"She can't sing," I say, clearing the table, and then put on my jacket for school. "She can't even hear."

"That may be," my mother says, "but she's going to try out anyway and I told Aunt Sara that you would go with her to tryouts."

I kiss my parents good-bye. I even kiss Benjamin who has spilled his orange juice all over our tiger cat, Sweeney, who is under the kitchen table and leave for school in time to meet Lucy at the corner of 36th and Macomb streets.

I have known Lucy Bressler since we were babies and she always astonishes me.

CHAPTER

2

Lucy, as I told you, was born deaf but no one knew it. Not even her mother and father who should have been the first to notice but Lucy wouldn't let them. It wasn't intentional on her part. She probably didn't even know she was missing something. But the fact is she has too much personality. That's what my mother has told me and also Lucy's mother, whom I call Aunt Sara even though she isn't my real aunt. When Lucy was a baby she was so friendly, so excited to see people, and so affectionate that everyone simply thought she was a happy-go-lucky regular girl who was slow to make sounds.

"She seemed to understand everything we were

saying to her," my mother said. "I'd take you over to play and you'd sit in the sandbox in the Bresslers' backyard babbling away with Lucy as if you knew exactly what was on her mind."

I imagine there is much more on Lucy's mind than she can tell anyone about since she got to be thirteen and people at Marywood, especially the seventh-grade girls, have turned cruel overnight. But when we were little, Lucy didn't need to talk for me to understand her. I simply did.

She was just over a year old when her parents found out that she was deaf although they had suspected it. We were playing in the library at the Bresslers' house and their giant German shepherd, Panda Bear, knocked over a vase full of roses right on the rug where we were playing. When the vase fell over, I jumped up and began to cry. But Lucy continued to sit on the floor and play with the Fisher-Price toy family as if nothing whatsoever had happened. She didn't even look up when I started to cry. Now, of course, we know she didn't hear me crying.

"Lucy," Aunt Sara said. According to my mother, Lucy did not look up when her mother called her name.

"Lucy," Aunt Sara said again in a very loud voice. "Lucy look at me."

But Lucy simply sat there playing house with her Fisher-Price mother and baby.

"Pamela," Aunt Sara said to my mother. "Do you see what has happened?"

My mother nodded. Even I knew something was the matter and I was only a baby.

Aunt Sara picked Lucy up from the floor. I don't remember, of course, but apparently she sat on a rocking chair and cried into Lucy's OshKosh overalls, while Lucy played happily on her lap as if nothing had happened.

And that was the beginning of the bad news for Lucy Bressler but you'd never know it from Lucy.

I live four blocks from Lucy on Cathedral Avenue in the house where I was born. It's a row house painted white with blue shutters and, in the summer, my mother fills the window boxes in the front with pink geraniums. Inside, however, the house is a little worn out. Brewster, our golden retriever, peed on the rug in the living room when he was a puppy before I was born, and now that he's old he's doing it again so the house, especially if it's raining, smells like a sewer. The chairs in the dining room are broken—the arms are off or the backs are cracked. At dinner we have to sit carefully. My mother keeps saying she will get around to gluing them but she hasn't the time. Sweeney sleeps on the rose velvet couch, covering the arms and seat with tiger hair, and the hall ceiling fell in and we can't fix it until the plumber finds the leak in the bathroom above it. All in all the house is sort of a mess ever since my mother got to be a lawyer and Benjamin was born.

"What do I smell?" my friends say when they come in the front door. Especially Lucy whose sense of smell is particularly good. She crinkles up her nose every time, as if she hasn't been in my house for years, and says in her funny foghorn voice, "What smells bad?"

My mother has promised that in the summer we will completely redo the house and that we might, if she and my father have a very successful year, put in a swimming pool. But I know better than that. In June she'll get a new case at work. She'll put geraniums in the window boxes, put off the redecoration until fall, and that will be that.

Lucy lives in a perfect brick house which smells of cinnamon cookies and potpourri.

"Your house is a mess," Lucy says to me. "Let's go to my house."

I never used to worry about the looks of things

until I turned thirteen, but now I worry about everything.

This morning Lucy is standing on the corner of 36th and Macomb streets in her new jean skirt which she got for her birthday, black tights and a black turtleneck. I notice these things lately. I also notice that ever since I started to get fat, everyone else is getting skinny, including Lucy. Her mother has fixed her hair, which is blond and frizzy-out-of-control, so it looks like a yellow halo around her head. I don't believe my mother has fixed my hair since Benjamin was born.

"Hello Eliza," she says brightly.

Lucy speaks well for a deaf person. I actually can understand what she says most of the time and so can people who don't know her well if they listen hard. Her parents insisted that she learn to talk and to understand people by reading their lips. They refused to let her learn sign language. They wanted her to be a perfectly ordinary girl in a regular school. Sometimes it works and sometimes it doesn't. It isn't easy.

"Hi," I say. We fall into step. She has a pocket full of chocolate-chip cookies and offers me one.

"You look pretty," she says, which is not true.

My complexion looks like a chocolate-chip cookie and the rest of me looks like a Tonka truck, especially in these blue jeans. But Lucy always says I look pretty.

"I'm fat," I say.

"Yes," Lucy agrees solemnly. "You're a little fat but that's okay." I like it better when she tells me lies.

"So," she says happily. "I'm going to try out for an orphan."

"Why?" I ask.

I am honest with Lucy. Most of the time I tell her the truth although I am the only one in the whole of Marywood Elementary who tells her the truth including the teachers. Mostly it's "Oh Lucy, you're so smart, you're so athletic, you're so gorgeous, you're so this, and you're so that," as if she's breakable, which she's not.

I decided a long time ago, when Lucy was first allowed to try a regular school in the third grade, that if her parents want her to live in an ordinary world she'd better find out what an ordinary world is like.

"I want to be an orphan," she says matter-of-factly.

"But you can't sing," I say.

She looks perplexed. "I can sing," she says.

I shrug. "I haven't heard you," I say.

"*To-mor-row, to-mor-row,*" she shouts in her very strange voice. "*I love ya to-mor-row.*"

"Well," I say, shaking my head. "Are you sure you want to try out?"

"Sure," Lucy says. "You'll be Annie and I'll be an orphan."

The sign-up sheet for *Annie* tryouts is on the bulletin board outside the principal's office. Lucy hands me a pencil to sign up.

Eddie Meyers is standing there with Sasha Brewer, his girlfriend for the week, and Louisa Peale, who wants to be Annie, and Vicki Sinkler, who thinks she's the cat's meow, as my mother would say. When Lucy writes her name down on the tryout sheet, they burst out laughing.

"I suppose she's going to sing," Sasha says, but of course Lucy can't hear her because she's writing her name on the bulletin board and her back is to them.

"Ask her," I say coolly.

When Lucy turns around, they have stopped laughing.

"Are you trying out for Annie?" Louisa Peale asks in her artificial sugar voice.

"No," Lucy says, innocent of their unkindness. "I'm trying out for an orphan."

"Great," Vicki says. "You'd make a great orphan."

We walk towards our lockers on the second floor next to the library.

"Didn't you sign up?" Lucy asks me, putting her books in her locker.

"I'll sign up later," I say. But it's not true. I've changed my mind about trying out for Annie. Let Louisa Peale, queen of the fakes, be Annie. I don't want to try out for anything.

3

The Marywood Elementary musical is performed the second weekend of March and has been every year of my lifetime. It is the most important event of the year in my neighborhood of Toledo, Ohio, including Christmas when there's a pageant at the Methodist Church and the Fourth of July when there's a parade.

First off, it takes six months to plan—not just for Mr. Blake who is the director and Ms. Gray who plays the piano—but for all of the parents and all of the children in the Marywood suburb of Toledo. Everyone is involved, including my grandmother who makes costumes, and Mr. Fate at the 7-Eleven who contributes soft drinks, and the librarian who organizes the pot luck dinners.

I can't describe to you the popularity for the girl chosen to be the lead. Last year, when we did *The Sound of Music*, it was Mary Dwyer, who has large violet eyes, a perfect slender figure, and black hair to her waist—all that besides a good voice. Now, no one in the whole suburb of Marywood will ever forget Mary Dwyer.

Her picture was on the front of the *Marywood Weekly* and on the second page of the arts section of the Toledo Sunday paper. She was invited to the mayor's Christmas party and when the governor of Ohio came to Toledo, she was chosen to represent Marywood Elementary at the reception in his honor. The Kiwanis Club gave her an award and Brassy's Department Store offered her a job modeling back-to-school fashions this September.

Ever since I can remember, since I started at Marywood Elementary in kindergarten, I have dreamed that in seventh grade I would be chosen for the lead in the musical. Everyone tells me I have the best voice in the class. At least, according to my father who is not generous with compliments, I have the loudest.

I used to practice "Do Re Mi" in the fifth grade, when Mary Dwyer was the lead in *The Sound of Music*; and "I'm Flying," in the fourth grade, when Sally Truman played Peter Pan; and "Hello,

Dolly!" in the third grade when Elaine Ross played the lead in *Hello, Dolly!* I knew all the words to all of the songs in my sleep. Every afternoon of October and November and December—with time out for the Christmas pageant in which I always, no matter what, play one of the shepherds—and every day of January and February during the months of daily rehearsals, I practiced in front of the mirror in my bedroom while Lucy Bressler sat on my bed, a little bored, I'm sure, but willing to be an audience for music she could not hear.

"You have a wonderful voice," Lucy would tell me earnestly when I finished a particular song in front of the mirror.

"How do you know I have a wonderful voice?" I'd say to her. That's the way I talk to her. I tell her the truth and usually it makes her laugh. Lucy was the only person willing to listen to me practice. Certainly my father wouldn't; he's always too busy. "Not now," we say in our family, imitating my father. "Later. Too busy right now." And certainly not Jacob or my mother who is always doing something dull with Benjamin if she's not in her office. Only Lucy who doesn't even know how good a singer I am.

Which I am. Everyone, even Sasha Brewer, who stands next to me in chorus and is the director's pet angel as well as being drop-dead beautiful, tells me I'll have the lead in the musical this year.

"Eliza for Annie," they shout on the playground, after school and during lunch. Everyone, that is, except Louisa Peale who has it in mind to be Annie herself and suggested Miss Hannigan for me because, as she said, "You look like Miss Hannigan." I don't know whether or not you remember Miss Hannigan, but if I do look like her I ought to retire from the human race today.

By the beginning of September when it was announced in assembly and then in the *Marywood Weekly* that we were going to do *Annie*, I should have been ready and waiting to be the most popular girl in Marywood and recognized on the streets of Toledo, Ohio, as well known. But something has happened to me since June and I don't recognize the person inside my skin. Some days I want to be Annie and some days I want to disappear.

Even at home the subject since September 9 when the musical was announced is *Annie* and will I get the lead.

"You'll never be an opera singer," my father says to me one night at dinner, "but you have a powerful voice and you can keep a tune."

"She can be an opera singer if she wants to," says my mother, who believes to her bones that, especially if you happen to be a girl, you can be anything you want to be.

"Eliza doesn't want to be an opera singer," Jacob says, bored by the endless conversation about the musical. "She wants to be famous."

Some of our family's worst conversations take place during dinner but this time I don't let Jacob make me furious and storm away from the table in disgust as I usually do. This time I say, "That's right. I want to be famous."

The next morning, walking to school with Lucy, I ask her if she understands the meaning of the word fame.

Lucy takes what I say to her very seriously. She pays attention and wants to understand.

"I understand," she'll say to me about anything I might be telling her.

"Do you really understand?" I'll ask.

"Yes," she'll nod. "I understand."

But the fact is, there are things that deaf children don't understand, especially about relationships and how people can be unkind. She doesn't understand, for example, that a girl like Louisa Peale with her sunshine smile can say terrible things about a person behind their back. Lucy understands hitting because she can see what is going on. But she doesn't understand the cruelty of girls because often it's practiced in secret. She expects an outside world in which people wish her well like the world with the Bresslers and her grandparents and aunts and uncles and cousins or even like my house in spite of Jacob. But the world of the seventh grade at Marywood Elementary is not as kind as it used to be when we were in sixth grade. This year, since the announcement of the musical in September, the seventh-grade girls, particularly, have been like "snakes" as Jacob would call them. "There's poison on their tongues."

And Lucy doesn't even recognize the change.

"Fame," Lucy says as we walk down Mulberry Street to the light. "I don't know about fame."

"Like *People* magazine," I say. "The people in *People* are in the magazine because they are famous and lots of people read it and recognize them."

"Right," Lucy says.

"And if you get to be in the musical at Marywood, especially if you get to be the lead, then you're famous. Not all over the world," I say reasonably. "But at least in Marywood and maybe in Toledo."

"Right," Lucy says. "So you will be famous."

I shrug. "If I get the lead."

"You'll get the lead," Lucy says. She takes a

bag of Doritos out of her pocket and we walk the rest of the way to Marywood Elementary eating.

"I want to be famous too," Lucy says.

"You are famous," I tell her. "You're famous because you're deaf. You're the only deaf person at Marywood Elementary and everyone knows who you are."

I don't want to hurt Lucy's feelings but it's perfectly true. Everyone at Marywood from the kindergarten up knows Lucy because she's different. But when I tell her this, she is not pleased.

"I want to be famous and not deaf," she tells me in her foghorn voice.

It's hard to argue with her. I'd rather be famous than deaf, too.

That night at dinner, I told my parents what Lucy had said and we all laughed but it didn't occur to me until today, when Lucy signed up to try out for the musical, that she is serious about fame and that she understands exactly that fame at Marywood Elementary means a part in the musical.

It is four and a half hours before tryouts and I am sitting in literature class which is first period after homeroom. We are discussing *Huckleberry Finn* which I have not read. Last night when my father went to the hospital to deliver a baby and my mother went to a PTA meeting, Jacob and Benjamin and I made popcorn and watched two programs on TV before the car announcing my mother's return turned into the driveway. Then I talked to Eddie Meyers about Sasha's birthday— a subject in which I have no interest but I have a great interest in Eddie Meyers and so I pretend. Then it was eleven-thirty and I went to bed without reading a page of *Huckleberry Finn*.

So I'm sitting in the front row of literature class trying to act as if I've read *Huckleberry Finn*, when Lucy bursts into the classroom from tutoring.

"Eliza," she calls out. "At recess you can teach me 'To-mor-row, to-mor-row.' "

"You bet," I say, glad to be saved from *Huckleberry Finn*.

And everyone in the class, including Ms. Carroll who is supposed to act like a grown-up, buries her head in a copy of *Huckleberry Finn* and laughs.

The thing about Lucy is that she doesn't seem to mind people laughing at her. I would die of embarrassment but she just smiles her sunny smile and just now, as the bell rings, she is singing "To-mor-row, to-mor-row" as if she has the voice of a bluebird. She's amazing.

CHAPTER

4

Until this year, I have had a happy childhood without the sort of bad luck Lucy had or even bad news, except that my grandmother who lived in Cleveland died when I was four. In third grade, I broke my ankle falling off my bike and in fifth grade, my father ran over a squirrel on Mulberry Street, and a clear picture of the dead squirrel stuck in my mind. Even now I sometimes have squirrel nightmares. But the fact is I've never been tested in an emergency, as Jacob has told me—as if he's a regular survivor of emergency tests. So I don't know how I'd be if, for example, I was born deaf.

I have practiced being Lucy. I stuffed cotton in my ears for a full day but I could still hear sounds through the cotton and of course I knew I could take the cotton out. I've thought about what it must be like not to hear music or the sound of your mother's voice or your own. What it must be like to have to look at someone's face every second in order to understand what is being said to you, and how much of real conversation Lucy must miss, and how it's dangerous to ride a bike in the street because you can't hear the cars or the door-bell or the telephone or the alarm clock, which in Lucy's case is attached to the bed and gives her a jolt to wake her up.

But usually I didn't give a lot of thought to troubles until this summer when, out of the blue, my life changed. I don't have any idea what happened to me.

My mother says it's my age. At the end of sixth grade, I was, I suppose, as my mother described me, a sunny and successful child. And then by July, it was as if I had been attacked by a terrible virus or swallowed a mind-altering pill. Every morning of the summer, usually my favorite time of the year, I woke up in a bad temper. By the time I got up everyone had already eaten breakfast so I'd go downstairs, make myself two or three bowls of cereal, have a donut if there was one in the fridge or an English muffin with tons of butter, and lie in the hammock in the backyard. By the Fourth of July, all of my shorts were too tight.

There were summer activities I was supposed to be doing, of course. I had voice lessons three times a week with Miss Kirby and swim club at noon and soccer camp in the afternoon, but I skipped four voice lessons in a row in July and Miss Kirby cancelled the rest of my lessons, telling my mother she did not have time to waste on me.

"I thought you loved to sing," my mother said to me. "I thought it was your favorite thing to do and that you wanted to be ready for the musical in the fall."

"I do," I said to her solemnly. "I just don't like Miss Kirby."

So my mother allowed me to change to Mrs. Grace. Mrs. Grace directs the Methodist Church Children's Choir and has a reputation for being wonderful with girls but she was certainly not wonderful with me. After the third lesson, to which I went in Jacob's baseball uniform since everything I owned was too tight to button, Mrs. Grace called my mother and said this summer was not the one for me to take voice lessons.

That afternoon, my mother called Aunt Jane who is her older sister. Aunt Jane has raised three teenagers—two badly, one well—but my mother says it's not Jane's fault about the two bad children. I sat on the steps and listened to their conversation in the kitchen and it went like this.

"Tell me Jane, how was Linden when she turned thirteen?"

Today, Linden is a model child, first in her class in high school, a great athlete, great this and great that, which is a lucky thing since her two brothers are practically in jail.

"The problem is this," my mother said. "Eliza seems depressed. She doesn't go to voice lessons. She's gaining weight eating junk food. She mopes around the house and is mean to Benjamin. And she doesn't like any of her old friends in school, except Lucy Bressler."

The conversation went on and on as my mother's conversations with Aunt Jane have a tendency to do, but the conclusion was that my mother should call Lucy's mother and find out if the same thing was happening to Lucy.

I didn't need to sit on the steps and listen to that because I knew very well that nothing is happening to Lucy. She is the same happy-go-lucky girl. Maybe it's a good thing to be deaf because you miss some things worth missing.

Like Dolly Page. I'd like to miss Dolly Page a lot. She used to be one of my close friends but now she's gotten stuck-up and wears makeup and collects pictures of boys which she pins all over the inside of her locker. I still like Mary Sawyer but she won't do anything at all, even go to the drugstore, unless Dolly goes along. And Tricia Bates has a boyfriend in eleventh grade—although he doesn't know about his good fortune even though she spent the summer in a royal blue bikini at the swimming club where he works. I don't need to tell you how I'd look in a bikini if I did have a boyfriend. You can imagine and it's not a pretty sight. So that's the story of my four best friends since second grade. Except Lucy.

"What has gotten into you Eliza?" my mother asked the other night when she came in to kiss me good night.

"Who knows?" I said in a not-very-pleasant voice. "Maybe a bacteria."

The fact is something has gotten into me and I can't seem to get whatever it is to leave.

"I hate myself," I said to Lucy one afternoon in early September when she had agreed to come home with me after school in spite of our bad-smelling house.

"You hate yourself?" Lucy asked, perplexed.

"I don't like the way I look and I've turned stupid when I used to be smart." I flopped down on my back on my blue-carpeted floor and put my feet on the *fleur-de-lis* wallpaper.

"You are only a little stupid in math," Lucy said matter-of-factly. "And you have zits."

"Right," I said miserably, covering my face with my arm. "Thousands of them."

"And I don't," Lucy said matter-of-factly.

Lucy tells the truth exactly as it occurs to her. If Dolly Page or Mary Sawyer were to tell me that I had zits all over my face and they didn't, I would have daydreams of pulling out their hair, knowing they were pleased with my bad luck. But Lucy believes exactly what she sees. She doesn't understand the complicated and competitive life of girls in the seventh grade.

"I don't like myself or Dolly or Tricia," I said to Lucy.

"You don't like Dolly and Tricia?" Lucy asked.

"I don't like them because they're so conceited. And I hate myself because I'm fat."

"What is conceited?" Lucy asked.

One of the nice things about Lucy is that I can tell her anything. She never makes a judgment.

I walked around my bedroom with my nose in

the air, waggling my hips. "Like that." I said. "Stuck-up."

Lucy walked around behind me imitating my walk.

"I love Dolly and Tricia," she said when I lay down on the bed.

"Even though they're stuck-up?" I asked.

She nodded. "But you are my best friend," she said happily.

I love Lucy but it sometimes drives me crazy that she's deaf. She doesn't know some of the things that are important. For example, she misses the changes in the seventh-grade girls which, I suppose, is the real reason for my unhappiness. My childhood is disappearing. The friends who used to be simple dependable friends like Mary and Tricia and Dolly are not simple or dependable any longer. Only Lucy.

5

Louisa Peale is practicing for *Annie* in the girls' room on the second floor next to the library. She is standing in front of the mirror with her blond hair frizzed in a circle around her head, making her eyes wide, singing, "The sun'll come out—to-mor-row." On the floor Mary Sawyer and Dolly are watching her with total admiration.

They give me a look when I come into the girls' room on my way to recess where I'm supposed to be practicing with Lucy, which I'm sure you know is the very last thing I want to do. I don't know what the look is supposed to mean but my guess is that they are telling me to be quiet and not interrupt the great singer/actress Louisa Patricia Peale. So I go into a cubicle, lock the door, and Louisa stops flat on the words "Bet your bottom dollar."

"Eliza," she calls in the sweet singsong voice she has developed to cover up for the fact that she's a born-again witch. "I didn't notice your name on the tryout sheets."

"That's because I didn't put it there," I say from my place in the cubicle.

"You didn't?" Dolly says, full of drama as usual. "I can't believe it."

"Why not?" Mary Sawyer is a much nicer person than Dolly, but boring because, as my mother says, sweet as she is Mary doesn't have a mind of her own.

"I'm too busy," I say from my cubicle.

"Too busy to be Annie?" Louisa asks.

"You'll be Annie, Louisa," Dolly says quickly.

"I'm sure you'll get Annie," Mary agrees. "Don't you think Louisa's awesome, Eliza?"

What I think, of course, is that Louisa is awful in spite of her quite good voice but I don't say that. "Awesome," I say.

I'm just about to open the door to leave before Dolly, who knows very well I've been rehearsing for the lead in the musical since I was seven years old, asks me why in the world I've decided not to try out, when Louisa brings up Lucy.

"Did you see that Lucy Bressler signed up for the musical?" she asks.

"She did?" Mary says.

"I didn't think she could sing," Dolly says.

"Eliza's teaching her," Louisa says. "Aren't you Eliza? She's planning to teach Lucy to sing by two o'clock this afternoon."

"Good luck," Dolly says.

I don't say anything. I button my pants, pull down my sweatshirt over my new wide hips which grew this summer, and am just pushing the door open when Sasha tumbles into the girls' room.

"You are not going to believe this," she says, "but Lucy's trying out for the musical."

Off and on since first grade, kids in the class have teased Lucy because she's different and kids are like that.

"People are afraid of differences," my mother said to me once when I asked why some children were unkind to Lucy. "They don't know how to behave around people who are not exactly like them. They are even uncomfortable around someone who has had a misfortune."

"Normal is how they should act," I said.

"Of course," my mother said. "That is how they should act, but instead they sometimes act as if bad luck or a handicap is catching. Lucky for Lucy that she's the girl she is."

Lucy is Miss Normal. Gradually, through the years, at Marywood people have gotten used to her peculiar voice and have learned to understand her flat way of talking. Besides, she has so much personality you often forget she's deaf. Until lately with the seventh-grade girls. But I've told you that already.

I'm late to meet Lucy on the playground but I'm so angry about what I heard in the girls' room that instead of going to my locker, I walk into the office of Mr. Blake, the director of the musical, who is sitting at his desk wearing a mushroom-colored beret as usual and pulling on the triangle of beard at the end of his chin. Mr. Blake, according to my mother, is the only truly unusual person in Toledo, Ohio. My mother tends to exaggerate so I don't know if he is the only one but he is certainly unusual. He is an extremely small man, the size of a child, actually, although not a dwarf. And the reason he is a director of plays at an elementary school instead of an actor, which is what he wanted to be, is that he is too small to play any roles but those of a child. Now that he is old, almost sixty I suppose, he can no longer play the role of a child. He has a gray beard, gray hair which he grows to his shoulders, and he always wears T-shirts with lines from the Marywood musicals. Today he has on a navy blue T-shirt with *Easy Street! Easy Street!* written in red letters.

"Hello, hello, hello, Eliza," he says when I knock on his door. "You are just the person I wanted to see. Why didn't you sign up to try out for *Annie?*"

"Actually, Mr. Blake," I say, "I came to see you about something else."

"Would you like a cigarette?" he asks. That's the kind of unusual my mother means. He is always asking, "Would you care for a cigarette, or a glass of red wine, or chocolate milk mixed with cyanide?" as if it's the most natural conversation in the world to have with a seventh-grader.

"Yes, please," I say. He offers me an imaginary cigarette, lights it, and we both pretend to smoke while I tell him about Lucy.

"Of course I'll audition Lucy, just like everyone else," Mr. Blake says.

"But she can't sing," I say, as if I am delivering surprising news.

"Then," Mr. Blake says seriously, "she won't get a part if she can't sing. Right? Right."

"The kids, especially the girls, are making fun of her. That's what I mean. I don't want her to be humiliated. And she really thinks she can sing."

"Good for her," Mr. Blake says. "Good, good, good for her. Maybe this afternoon, she'll sing like a bird. Remember *The Little Engine That Could.* 'I think I can, I think I can.' Another cigarette?"

"No thank-you," I say.

"And what about you?" he asks.

"What do you mean?"

"You're a different kind of engine, Eliza Westfield. Right? Right. 'I think I can't. I think I can't. I think I can't.' "

I laugh in spite of myself. "I have a very busy year this year," I say. "I'm taking soccer after school."

"I see," Mr. Blake says, pulling his beret down over one eye. "And you were never very much interested in the musicals here, isn't that right?" Of course Mr. Blake knows better since he has known me very well since I was five and a half.

"Well," I start to say but he is not going to stop for conversation.

"You have never liked singing either and certainly you never wanted to be the lead. Such a lot of responsibility. You might forget your lines or throw up on stage." He pretends to take a glass out of his drawer and pours me red wine. "I understand completely. You're the kind of student who wants to be in charge of refreshments. I'll keep that in mind," he says.

I get up to leave.

"I remember when you were in the third grade, Eliza," he says. "The year we did *Hello, Dolly!* and you, the size of a green pea, came to school dressed up as Dolly and in the lunchroom in front of everyone you sang, 'Hello, Dolly, well Hello, Dolly, it's so nice to have you back where you belong.' And I said to you, 'Wait until seventh grade.' Remember?"

I nod.

"And now it's seventh grade. Right?"

"Right," I say.

"So much for that girl. Out the window. Goodbye Eliza Westfield of old. Hello Eliza Westfield of new. Too bad. Too bad. Maybe I'll have to give the part of Annie to a boy."

"It happened this summer," I say sadly. "I just changed."

"Pity, pity," Mr. Blake says to me. "Pity, pity, pity. Cyanide for the road?" he asks.

"Sure," I say.

"Eliza," he calls just as I'm walking out the door. "There are a lot of good teachers at Marywood Elementary aren't there?" he asks.

I nod.

"In fact, most of them, wouldn't you say?" he asks.

I wouldn't say so but I don't tell Mr. Blake that news.

"But you know who is the best teacher I've seen here at Marywood in twenty-two years of sitting in this office and directing musicals?"

I shake my head.

"Lucy," he says. "Miss Lucy Bressler."

"What do you mean?" I ask.

"Well you might ask," he says, "because she doesn't teach math or literature and we certainly know she doesn't teach singing. So she must teach children. Right?"

"Right," I say, not understanding at all.

Sometimes Mr. Blake is simply too strange for a normal thirteen-year-old girl in a bad mood. I grab a sweater from my locker and run down the steps to meet Lucy who happens at this very moment to be practicing "To-mor-row, to-mor-row," in front of a small group of seventh-grade boys.

Lucy Bressler will do anything.

6

Lucy is a very pretty girl. Even Jacob agrees. She has green eyes speckled with brown, a small bright face, and curly blond hair which she changes as often as she changes clothes—which is often, sometimes three times a day. Today she's wearing it in a puffed ponytail on top of her head like a small yellow hat. Somehow, just the look of her is straight out of a magazine. Maybe *Seventeen*.

"To-mor-row, to-mor-row, I love ya to-mor-row," she's singing. I cannot really make out the words because she's singing so loud and in one key, so it sounds as if she's singing one single word and holding the note.

"Eliza," she calls when she sees me. When she says my name, it sounds like this: "I—Za."

"So," Eddie Meyers says to me as I walk past him. "I see you haven't signed up for the musical."

"Nope," I say.

"Me neither."

"Big surprise," I say. That's the way I talk to Eddie Meyers since I certainly don't want him to know that I like him.

"Looks like Lucy's going to get Annie," says Billy Miller who is standing next to Eddie, shoulder to shoulder, his hands in his pockets. Unlike Eddie who's an athlete first and last, Billy Miller will be in the musical, probably as Daddy Warbucks because of his voice which is good and very low. I don't know what's going to happen to Billy when his voice changes. Already, it's ten feet deep.

"I'd rather adopt Lucy than you, any day," Billy says.

You probably remember that Daddy Warbucks is the rich man who adopts Orphan Annie and already, of course, Billy knows he's going to get the part.

"My guess is you'll be adopting Louisa Peale," I say to Billy.

"What are you saying?" Lucy asks.

Unless Lucy is looking right at you so she can read your lips, she doesn't know what's going on. Actually she senses a lot even though she can't hear. But the fact is she just doesn't know everything that people mean and kids, of course, talk all the time and interrupt each other.

"Tell her we're talking about sex," Eddie Meyers says.

"Shut up, Eddie," I say. I don't know why I like Eddie Meyers. He's a terrible boy.

"Tell her we're talking about her wonderful singing voice," Billy Miller says. Billy is like Mary Sawyer, a follower. He's actually a very nice boy, even sweet, but if Eddie Meyers is around he will say absolutely anything to make Eddie laugh.

"I'll tell her you're a girl in disguise Billy," I say to him, walking down the hill with Lucy to the shed where she's going to practice for tryouts.

"What was everybody saying?" Lucy asks.

So I tell her word for word. I don't protect Lucy. I don't pretend to her that people say nice things when they don't, or that she has a good voice when she can't sing, or that she looks good in a skirt if it's too tight—she has one of those little bottoms that sticks out in a tight skirt.

Dolly is always shocked when she hears the way I talk to Lucy but I don't think I'm being unkind. My mother says that it's kind to Lucy to tell her the truth. After all, the Bresslers have decided she should live in a world of children who can hear instead of going to a school for the deaf so she may as well know the truth about things.

"Eddie Meyers said we were talking about sex," I say. "Which we weren't."

"He's cute," Lucy says.

"He's okay."

"But mean?"

"Yes, he's a little mean. And then Billy Miller said you have a wonderful voice."

Lucy smiles brightly.

"He was being sarcastic."

"Sarcastic?" Lucy's vocabulary is not great, of course, since she has to learn every single word without hearing it. Just the thought of how many words Lucy has had to learn by studying, that for the rest of us just slip in through our skin, makes me exhausted.

"Sarcastic is mean," I say.

"He thinks I sing terrible?" she asks.

"He thinks you can't sing," I say.

"How does it sound when I sing?" she asks me.

"Like this," I say. With my hand, I draw a straight line. "And it should sound like this," I say. And I move my hand up and down.

"You will teach me how to move my voice," she says.

"Yes," I say. "We'll work at it now and again after lunch."

"I don't have much time to learn to sing," Lucy says earnestly.

"That's right," I agree. "It's eleven o'clock now and you have about four hours."

We are standing behind the shed where the athletic equipment is kept and next to the basketball court. Some of the seventh- and eighth-grade boys are practicing basketball and a group of girls including Louisa Peale is sitting on the hill just beyond us but no one can actually see us behind the shed. I show Lucy how to stand and how to breathe.

"Now," I say. "You watch me and follow my hand with your voice. If it goes up, your voice goes up. If it goes down, your voice goes down. Now watch." First I sing, moving my hand with my own voice.

"To-mor-row, to-mor-row, I love ya to-mor-row."

"Now," I say to Lucy. "You try. Very slowly at first and watch my hand carefully."

"Are you going to be there when I try out?" Lucy asks.

"Of course," I say.

"Will you move your hands for me, up and down, so I can move my voice? I won't be able to remember when to go up and when to go down unless you're there."

"Of course," I say.

I can't believe myself lately. More than any-thing—more than a bicycle when I was seven, or an A on my report card for which I am paid five dollars, or even a trip to New York with just me and my mother, I want to be Annie. I can hear myself and I sound wonderful. My voice fills the gymnasium. But the real trouble is that I can see myself too and the person I see on the stage in a red wig playing Annie is awkward and uncoordi-nated and fat.

I simply don't have the nerve to try out and I hate myself for that.

"Okay," I say to Lucy.

"Okay," she agrees.

"To-mor-row, to-mor-row, I love ya to-mor-row."

She follows my hand carefully and her voice does move up and down. But it doesn't sound like singing and that makes me very sad.

Maybe, I think, as we walk back up the hill together, Lucy could be Annie and mouth the words and I could be backstage singing. I almost suggest this to Lucy when we bump into Mr. Blake carrying his cat, Bluster, under his arm and headed for the parking lot.

> "Eliza and Lucy,
> Lucy and Eliza,
> Such a lovely pair
> To greet an old man's
> eyes-a."

"What did he say?" Lucy asks.

"He's singing a song to us," I say to her.

"I'm taking Bluster home and putting him in his room without supper for peeing on my carpet," Mr. Blake says. "And then I'll be back at school in time for tryouts."

"Lucy," he grabs the fuzzy ponytail on the top of her head. "You are signed up to try out for *Annie?*"

"For an orphan," Lucy says.

"Good, good, good. And Eliza. Remember, if you're not signed up by three o'clock you don't have a second chance. You can't change your mind," he says, waving Bluster's paw at me. "Now or never. No special considerations."

"I know," I say.

"Do you have a cigarette I could have?" he asks.

"Sure," I say. I reach in my pocket and hand him an imaginary cigarette.

"Remember," he says to me, holding the pretend cigarette between his second two fingers. "This is the only brand of cigarette safe to smoke. I don't want to ever see you smoking anything else. Right?"

"Right," I say.

"What did you give him?" Lucy asks.

"A make-believe cigarette," I say.

"And what did he tell you?"

"He told me if I don't sign up before three o'clock to try out for the musical, I don't get a second chance."

"He's crazy," Lucy says.

"He's not crazy," I say. "That's the rule. It's always been the rule."

Lucy looks at me with a knowing look she sometimes gets when she understands more than I think she does.

"You are crazy not to try out," she says. "It's all you ever wanted to do."

I am surprised and very pleased that Lucy knows this about me but I try not to show it.

"Well," I say. "Sometimes things change."

The lunchroom is a zoo. I am late because Ms. Henderson kept me after class to correct the fifty-one I got on my math test last Friday. And then she has the nerve to ask me if there is anything I have to tell her. "No," I say. "I have absolutely nothing to tell you except that I am late for lunch." What does she expect? A confession about my private thoughts just because I didn't study for math?

"I flunked the test because I didn't study," I say, just to make sure she understands and doesn't tell the principal that something is going on with me and perhaps I should see a shrink. Eddie Meyers was kept after, too, because he hasn't done his math homework since September and we walk into the lunchroom together.

"What is going on?" he asks. "It's like a machine shop in here." He is right. The noise is incredible.

"The musical," I say, getting in line for the hot lunch although I don't feel like eating anything. "Everybody's nervous for tryouts."

"I guess so," he says, standing behind me in line. "Sasha's trying out for Miss Hannigan," he says. I don't say anything. Why should I pretend to be thrilled about Sasha as Miss Hannigan when I'm not? I tell myself. I used to be very polite. As short a time ago as last June.

In one corner of the lunchroom, Louisa Peale is sitting with Dolly Page and Mary Sawyer and a few of her other friends. And mine. All of them are looking at her and she is talking. I notice from my place in line that she has nothing for lunch at all except a carton of juice. I order myself two scoops of mashed potatoes and gravy, no meat, no vegetable, and chocolate milk.

"You'll get fat," Eddie says, ordering ravioli.

"Break my heart," I say, and carry my tray over to the table with Dolly and Mary and the perfect Louisa Peale. I've looked all over the cafeteria for Lucy and I don't see her.

"Hiya," Louisa says. "We're all freaked."

"It sounds like that," I say and sit down.

As soon as I sit down, I'm no longer interested in mashed potatoes and gravy. Instead, I have a terrible need to call my mother. I check the clock over the door. Twelve-thirty. That means she's out of meetings and in her office unless she has a lunch date. So I excuse myself from the table and cross the lunchroom towards the library where there is a telephone.

The sound in the lunchroom is escalating and what I hear as I walk between the long tables full of children is "Annie" and "Annie" and "Miss Hannigan" and "Billy Miller" and "Louisa" and "Eliza Westfield," a name I recognize as my own, but it is always peculiar to overhear your name spoken in a way that does not seem to belong to you. Several times I hear Lucy's name mentioned and I stop to look around once again. I'm a little worried not to see her here. She is always on time for everything.

The excitement in the room is moving out of control. Apparently Ms. Starling, who is in charge of the lunchroom for the month of October, agrees because she is tapping on the glasses for silence. *"Girls and boys!"* she shouts. I just barely hear her although I can tell she is shouting. *"Please. Quiet in the lunchroom."* There is no change and she stands up on a chair. By this time, I am on the other side of the lunchroom and suddenly afraid that I'm going to be sick, for which the immediate solution seems to be to hear my mother's voice on the other end of the telephone.

I like my mother. Everyone I know loves her mother, of course, but only a few of my friends like their mothers. Lucy, for one, and me. My mother is cheerful and funny, a little like a girl herself, even though she's over forty which is older than the mothers of most of my friends. She even looks like a girl. She is small and red-haired— and, well, funky. She wears suspenders and big shirts and short skirts with patterned tights. Not serious clothes at all, especially for a lawyer. But what I like best about my mother is that she listens to what I say and to what I really say. Like last night.

"I don't like Ms. Henderson," I said at dinner last night.

"You never like your teachers," my father said.

"The teachers at Marywood are creeps," Jacob said, coming to my defense, to my surprise.

"She likes as many of her teachers as you like of your patients," my mother said. My mother doesn't always take my side but I notice that she does when my father is in one of his "I know everything" moods, which must annoy her as much as it does me and Jacob. Benjamin is too young to be annoyed by anything but vegetables.

"I like all of my patients," my father said.

My mother raised her eyebrows. She didn't say anything or give any examples but I, for one, know my father doesn't like Mrs. Veronica Sale, whose baby isn't due until January but nevertheless calls him at home twice a week at least about pains she thinks she's having. And I'm sure there are more than Mrs. Sale.

"What don't you like about Ms. Henderson?" my mother asked me.

"I don't like that she's not fair," I said.

My father has a lecture about fairness, which he gives now: what is and what isn't fair, like life, for example. But I won't bother you with that lecture because it isn't particularly interesting.

Later last night my mother came into my bedroom, sat down on my bed, and played with my hair, which I love her to do.

"Did you do poorly on the math test Friday?" she asked.

"I flunked," I said.

"Because you didn't understand what was going on in math?" she asked.

"I flunked because I just hate Ms. Henderson," I said and we talked and talked into the night until I finally told her the truth. That I'm so busy worrying about how I look and how I feel that I don't even study for math tests or read my literature homework, or much else in school for that matter, which is why my grades have fallen into a well. She didn't exactly say "So what?" about my grades but she certainly didn't make me think that flunking a math test is the end of the world. So I went to sleep feeling much better for a change.

I dial my mother's office number and she answers the phone. She has a secretary who says "Ms. Westfield's office" when you call and sometimes I just like to call to hear her say "Ms. Westfield's office" because it makes my mother seem important, but I've never told her that. This time I'm glad she has answered herself because I'm suddenly too sick to stand up.

"Hi," I say weakly.

"Liza," my mother says. "What's the matter?"

"I'm sick," I say.

"Sick?" she asks. "Do you have the flu?"

"I don't know what I have," I say. "I feel terrible."

"Do you want to go home?" she asks.

"Can you come get me?" I ask.

"Of course," she says. "I can always come get you."

I hesitate. I certainly want to go home. The musical is making me sick. I know in my heart, as my mother would say, that I want to try out and also that I'd rather die than try out.

"Maybe I'd like you to come get me," I say.

The real problem is Lucy. I promised Lucy that I would help her try out and somehow I know I cannot let her down.

"Eliza?"

"What do you think I should do?" I say.

"I think you should go for a walk," my mother says. "Put on your jacket and go out to the playground, which is probably empty and the lunchroom is probably noisy with excitement about tryouts. Do that and if you don't feel any better in the next little while, call me."

"And you'll be there?" I ask.

"I'll be right here all day," she says.

I hang up the telephone and I don't go back to the lunchroom. Instead, I go up the stairs to my locker, put on my blue-jean jacket and go out the back door of Marywood Elementary to the playground.

It is a sunny bright October day, barely cool with a light breeze. Just the silence of the playground after the lunchroom is a relief. I walk across the basketball court, along the field where girls practice soccer, past the equipment shed and the tennis courts to the path which leads up to the top of the hill where there is a wonderful view of Toledo. But just as I pass the equipment shed, I hear a peculiar sound. As I go closer, it seems to be the sound of an animal, perhaps a raccoon, who has been locked in the equipment shed and is protesting.

It is not until I come around the corner that I realize the sound I hear is singing. There is Lucy, all by herself, singing "Tomorrow" at the top of her lungs.

CHAPTER

8

You can hear a pin drop in the auditorium where I am sitting, fourth row back in between Lucy and a girl called Sun Moo, who does not speak particularly good English but dances like an angel and gets straight A's. In the row in front of me sits Louisa Peale. She is alone. She is giving small waves to people as they come into the auditorium as if she has recently been crowned the Queen of Toledo. Sasha Brewer and Eddie Meyers are sitting at the end of the aisle where I am and it looks from where I'm sitting as if he's holding her hand. Billy Miller and Mary Sawyer are sitting together and Dolly comes in late after the bell. There are plenty of people in the auditorium, forty or more, but I don't want to bother you with the names of people you will not get to know in this story.

On the stage Mr. Blake, who has changed his beret to a white one with an artificial long-stemmed rose pinned on the back, is pacing up and down. Ms. Gray is here to accompany the tryouts on the piano and also the English teachers Ms. DuRoss and Mr. DeRosa who are going to help Mr. Blake.

"Hello, hello, hello," Mr. Blake says. "Welcome to the tenth annual Marywood Elementary School tryouts for the musical *Annie*." He changes from the formal posture in which he began his announcement to a clownish dance. "The sun'll come out—to-mor-row," he sings.

"The story is this," he begins. "There is Annie who lives in an orphanage with some other orphans—we'll have about twelve of them, five with speaking roles, all with singing and dancing roles. Then there's Miss Hannigan who runs the orphanage and is either despicable or not, depending on your point of view. I happen to love Miss Hannigan but I have a tendency to enjoy bad company." Mr. Blake is now sitting on the piano with Bluster, the cat, who apparently did not have to remain long in his room. "Miss Hannigan has the best song in the show."

He goes on to tell about Daddy Warbucks taking an orphan for Christmas and Grace, his secretary, and Miss Hannigan's brother and how it all ends up—what else—happily ever after. But you know the story and so does everyone else in the audience, wriggling nervously in their seats wishing for tryouts to begin and end pronto.

"What is he saying?" Lucy asks impatiently, but I put my finger to my lips.

"This is what I'm going to do," Mr. Blake says. "Listen carefully. Everything happens in a single day. No waiting all week with a stomachache to find out if you got the role you wanted. We may be sitting in this hot room without any air all night unless you're quiet so be pleasant, patient, and professional, please." This seems to amuse him. He plays a few notes on the piano and does a quick tap dance. "Dum de dum dum dedum," he says and sits up on the piano where he has left a piece of paper. "I have a list here of people trying out for *Annie.* Some of you have indicated to me the parts you want to play but I am paying very little attention to that. I may even cast a boy in the part of Annie." He does another tap dance and curtsies. I should tell you that the girls and boys in the auditorium are losing patience with his act.

"Here is the list," he says, sensing their impatience. "And I'm going straight down the twenty-seven names, one at a time. You will come up to the stage, tell Ms. Gray what song you have prepared for tryouts, stand facing the audience, where I will be, and sing until your heart breaks. After everyone on this list has had his/her turn, Ms. DuRoss, Ms. Gray, Mr. DeRosa and I, Mr. Blake, will meet backstage for forty-seven minutes to decide on the parts, during which time you can go to the cafeteria for a cup of hot chocolate with cyanide but there will not be time to have your appendix out so be prudent. We will then return to this auditorium and announce the cast. Then you can go home and dance or cry, do your homework, eat dinner and come back to school to-morrow, whatever the outcome of today, each and every one of you ready to put on the best musical Marywood has ever done."

I like Mr. Blake very much and he can be funny but, as you can imagine, this roomful of nervous kids waiting for the high moment of their lives at Marywood Elementary is not laughing at Mr. Blake now.

"Sasha Brewer," Mr. Blake calls out.

Sasha is what my brother Jacob calls a very put-together girl. Which is to say that if anything in the world ever bothers Sasha, you'd never know it. Today she has on jeans, a purple pullover sweater, and high-top bright pink tennis shoes. She looks, as always, beautiful, beautiful, beautiful, as Mr. Blake would say. Now she goes up to the piano and says something to Ms. Gray who begins to play "Easy Street" and Sasha, cool as ice and confident, breaks out into song. And dance. It is certainly clear she has been practicing night and day, and clear as well that she's got the role of Miss Hannigan in her back pocket—that's my father's expression. When she finishes singing, we all stand up and shout.

"No applause," Mr. Blake says. "No demonstration of approval or disapproval," he adds and I'm glad he's said something now because I'm worried about what will happen when it's Lucy's turn to sing.

After Sasha, there is Mary Ann Drake, Jessica Sage, Lizzie Parsky, Tracey Prayer, Charlotte Kilgray, Johanna Friedman, Sarahdale DeAngelis, Joshua Lake and Tommy Brown. But I'm not going into their performances which, with the exception of Sarahdale DeAngelis who will probably get the part of Molly, were just mediocre. That's my father's word too. It means not great and not terrible which is how my father feels about everything. He's a very even man, my mother says, but it doesn't look like I'm going to turn out to be much like him.

Billy Miller has just been called. It's not easy to be Billy Miller at this moment because most of his friends are boys like Eddie Meyers who would not be caught dead on stage except to accept an athletic award so Billy is going to be ridiculed. Which in fact is happening this very moment from the back of the room where a group of boys have come into the auditorium and are starting to hiss.

Mr. Blake, who is, as I've mentioned, a very small man, has a temper and when he loses it people pay attention.

"Out of here," he says now. He doesn't even shout and they leave.

Louisa is next.

"Oh no," she squeals. "I'm so scared. Wish me luck, luck, luck," she says brushing hands with her friends as she passes them, walking out from the middle of the row where she has been sitting. She runs up to the stage on her little girl feet, trying to look like a ten-year-old orphan instead of a thirteen-year-old young woman, as my father calls girls with breasts.

Louisa is good. I have to admit, she's very good. For a moment, a very short moment, followed by a severe case of butterflies, I wish I had signed up. I want to beat her because it's certain that she has no competition for Annie except me, unless they can find another Molly to make Sarahdale Annie. And now I'm going to have all year until March for Louisa Peale to be unbearable as Annie and famous.

Margaret Hansen is next and then Lisa Olson and Tommy Herz and Maggie Bausch and Courtney Blakemore. And then Lucy.

"My turn?" Lucy asks when Mr. Blake calls her name. She has been concentrating on his face the whole time he speaks.

"Your turn," I say.

My job is to go down to the front row and move my hand up and down with the notes while she's singing, but in such a way that the students sitting behind me don't see what I'm doing.

"I'm going to sing without the piano," Lucy says in her very loud voice so everyone can hear, and behind me there is some laughter.

"She sings so well she doesn't need a piano?" Allison Braveman asks.

"She doesn't hear the piano, dodo," I say.

"Then why is she trying out for a musical?" Allison asks.

Mr. Blake, I'm glad to say, asks Allison to leave the auditorium and while she is leaving, I move down to the front and sit down to the left of the piano so Lucy can see me.

She stands up at the front of the stage, half facing the audience where the rest of the teachers are sitting down the row from me, and half facing Mr. Blake who has moved his stool to the wings.

"What are you going to sing, Lucy?" he asks her.

" 'Tomorrow.' " Lucy says.

My heart is beating so fast I feel it in my mouth the size of a Ping-Pong ball.

"Whenever you're ready," Mr. Blake says.

"Ready," Lucy says. She turns just slightly so she can see me and then she begins.

"The sun'll come out—to-mor-row," she sings. I am moving my hand but I can't keep up with the words so sometimes her voice is up when it ought to be down and down when it ought to be up, but as I've said already there isn't much difference anyway. My stomach is shaking and I am perspiring as if it's the middle of August. I think I am going to stop breathing at any moment and I wonder if that happens will I die.

Lucy knows the words to the song perfectly. She sings each one carefully and stands with her hands folded, a small smile at the corner of her lips. She looks just wonderful and something is happening to the audience behind me. I can feel it happening. A change in the room, a silence. When she has finished singing, the minute she stops, everyone is standing up and clapping and cheering. I am clapping and cheering, too. I think I'm going to cry. Lucy runs off the stage to hug me.

"Was I good?" she asks. She is so excited she's jumping up and down. "Everyone is clapping so I must have been good," she says.

I ruffle her frizzy hair.

"Did I sing?" she asks, but she doesn't wait for me to answer. "Do you think I'll be an orphan?"

In a way, I wish this were the end of the story because everyone in the auditorium is still clapping. But as it will turn out, the story has quite a different end.

"Thank you, Lucy," Mr. Blake says. "Mary Sawyer. Ready?"

And Mary Sawyer goes up on stage.

Mary is not very good at singing but she's a good actress, uninhibited, and she dances extremely well. After Mary is Tom Folger and Elizabeth Shields and Jim Johnson and Robert Healy. Then Hannah and Benjamin Richards who are twins.

I am feeling very relaxed. Lucy has finished and the day of tryouts is almost over. In fact when Mr. Blake says "Eliza Westfield" I am thinking of the chocolate-chip sundae I am going to make when I get home. Although I hear my name and it sounds familiar, I don't react at first.

"Eliza," Mr. Blake says.

I look up.

"Yes?"

"Your turn."

"My turn?" I say. The bottom falls out of me, exactly as if I'm a broken jar of jam, or that's how it feels.

"I didn't sign up," I say.

"Your name is Eliza Westfield?"

There is laughter behind me.

"And this says Eliza Westfield."

He comes to the end of the stage and shows me the sign-up sheet with my name in my writing. I look at the name. Eliza Westfield. My handwriting exactly. I wonder, I think, did I actually sign up? Did I go to the bulletin board sometime after recess and sign up and yet have no memory of doing it?

"Well?" Mr. Blake asks.

There is a moment, a small moment, in which the auditorium is silent. In that moment—I don't remember making a decision. I don't remember a single thought going through my head or even a feeling of anxiety. It is almost too sudden for anxiety. And then I am standing up, walking past Lucy and Ms. DuRoss and Mr. DeRosa and Mary Sawyer and Dolly. I am up on the stage.

"What will you sing?" Ms. Gray asks me as if it's the most normal and expected thing in the world for me to be standing here.

" 'Tomorrow,' " I say.

I know all of the songs so well I could sing them in my sleep. I have practiced them forever but just now I don't even remember the names of them except "Tomorrow" and that's only because I have practiced it all day with Lucy.

"The sun'll come out—to-mor-row," I begin.

There are other tryouts after me. A lot. I don't remember. After I try out, I sit back in the front row, slump down in my seat, and pray although I am not a person who prays except in an emergency. "Please, dear Lord," I say, "give Annie to Louisa Peale. Just this once. I will do anything," I say.

Lucy is very quiet. After Mr. Blake and Mr. DeRosa and Ms. DuRoss and Ms. Gray leave the room, she asks me if I want to go to the library with her and I say, "No." I think I am going to be sick.

"Do you think I will get an orphan?" she asks.

"I hope," I say.

"I hope you get Annie," she says.

"I hope Louisa does," I say.

Mr. Blake is out of the room for forty-seven minutes exactly by the clock and when he comes back no one in the auditorium has moved from his seat. There's been conversation but it has been subdued and when he walks onto the stage with the list in his hand, there is absolute silence.

"Quiet, quiet, quiet," he says, although there is no sound.

"Quiet, quiet, quiet," he says again and there's a nervous giggle just behind me. "Quiet," he begins.

Orphans:	Margaret Hansen
	Louisa Peale
	Courtney Blakemore
	Hannah Richards
	Mary Sawyer
	Elizabeth Shields
	Jessica Sage
	Lizzie Parsky
	Charlotte Kilgray
	Mary Ann Drake
Molly:	Sarahdale DeAngelis
Miss Hannigan:	Sasha Brewer
Rooster:	Jonathan Schade
Daddy Warbucks:	Billy Miller
Grace:	Dolly Page
Annie:	Eliza Westfield
Stage Manager:	Lucy Bressler

"Eliza." Everyone is shouting.

"Liza. Eliza. Eliza Westfield."

I hear them but I cannot turn around. I cannot even stand up.

Suddenly Lucy is hugging me and hugging me.

"You got Annie," she's saying. "Aren't you happy?"

I can't even talk.

"Did I get an orphan?" she asks me. "He read my name. I saw him read my name."

"Not an orphan, Lucy." My voice is almost too thin for sound but she can see what I'm saying.

"Not an orphan?" she asks.

I shake my head. "You got stage manager," I say. "Stage manager is important. It's the most important part of the play. You will run everything."

"But I won't sing," she says.

"You won't sing," I say and we have to stop talking because everyone is crowding around to congratulate me.

Lucy and I don't walk straight home. Instead we go to Billy's Best Ice Cream Store at the end of Mulberry Street and I order a double scoop chocolate sundae with marshmallow sauce.

"Tomorrow I go on a diet," I say.

Lucy nods. "Good," she says. "Annie's not supposed to be very fat."

We sit at a small booth across from each other and I tell Lucy about stage manager and what an important job it is. She seems perfectly happy to be stage manager but I cannot believe after trying so hard that she isn't upset not to be an orphan. Lucy always surprises me.

"Lucy?" I ask.

"Yes," she says.

"Are you very upset not to be an orphan?"

She looks at me quizzically. "I can't sing," she says simply. "You told me I couldn't and you were right."

"But you tried so hard."

"I know," she shrugs.

"It's not fair," I say.

"I know," she agrees.

There is another thing I want to ask her in such a way that she will tell me the truth. I want to find out who signed me up for tryouts.

"Lucy," I say.

She has ordered Oreo cookie ice cream with jimmies and is licking off the jimmies first.

"Did you sign me up?"

"Mr. Blake did," she says.

"No," I shake my head. "Mr. Blake didn't. First he wouldn't because he's not that kind of man and second he doesn't know my handwriting. That handwriting had to be done by someone who knows me perfectly."

Lucy leans her chin in her hand.

"So, Lucy? Tell me the truth."

"Yes?" she asks.

"Why did you sign me up?"

She looks at me with this funny little smile she has.

"I signed you up because you wanted to be Annie," she says, taking a bite of my chocolate ice cream. "And now you are."